Karen Barbour

MR. BOWTIE

Harcourt Brace Jovanovich, Publishers

San Diego   New York   London

1991

To CARLYN!

much Love

DOT and GooD luck to you.

Karen

Library of Congress Cataloging-in-Publication Data
Barbour, Karen.
Mr. Bow Tie/Karen Barbour. — 1st ed.
p.   cm.
Summary: Two children and their parents befriend a homeless man living on the street and help him find his family.
ISBN 0-15-256165-X
[1. Homeless persons — Fiction.]   I. Title.
PZ7.B2336Mr   1991
[E] — dc20   90-24453

First edition   A B C D E

The paintings in this book were done in Winsor & Newton gouache and watercolors on 140-lb. T.H. Saunders cold-press paper.
The text type was set in Souvenir Light and the display type was set in Broadway Engraved by Thompson Type, San Diego, California.
Color separations by Bright Arts, Singapore
Printed and bound by Tien Wah Press, Singapore
Production supervision by Warren Wallerstein and Ginger Boyer
Designed by Camilla Filancia

To Bonnie, with thanks and admiration

—*K.B.*

A man lived in our neighborhood. He always wore funny clothes, and he never said a word to anyone.

He slept outside our store, and his only friend was a mouse. We called
him Mr. Bow Tie because . . .

he always wore a bow tie.

We saw him on dark, rainy days.

We saw him on hot, sunny days.

One day, our dad gave Mr. Bow Tie a big sandwich with a pickle and two root beers.

Mr. Bow Tie was so pleased he took our broom and swept the whole sidewalk spotlessly clean.

He *always* swept the sidewalk after that.

And he helped around the store a lot. Our dad gave him breakfast
and lunch — and dinner, too!

One day our dad took us downtown to a big office to try to find out who
Mr. Bow Tie really was. They told us his real name: Elliot Lyman Bristow.

He was a decorated war hero, and his mom and dad lived far away.
We sent a letter to them. Mom and Dad helped us write it.

Things went on as usual. When Mr. Bow Tie wasn't helping in the store,
he played games with us. But still he never spoke a word.

Then Mr. Bow Tie's mom and dad wrote a letter. They said they would be coming to see him *the next day!*

The next morning, my dad asked Mr. Bow Tie to come over to our apartment.

And he came.

He seemed surprised to be inside. He didn't say a word, but then . . .

we saw that he wanted to take a bath!

And so he did.

After that, he brushed his hair . . .

and shaved, and clipped his mustache.

We sewed a new button on his shirt, put new laces in his shoes, and . . .

our dad gave him a new coat . . .

and a bow tie!

That afternoon a little old man and a little old lady drove up to our store.

Mr. Bow Tie cried and hugged them both as hard as he could.

Then all of us gave him a going-away present.

He got in the car with his mom and dad, and as they drove away,
Mr. Bow Tie leaned out and shouted so loud:

"Good-bye, and thanks a million!"